Sheltie in Danger

Make friends with

Sheltie

The little pony with the big heart

Sheltie is the lovable little Shetland pony with a big personality. He is cheeky, full of fun and has a heart of gold. His best friend and new owner is Emma, and together they have lots of exciting adventures.

Share Sheltie and Emma's adventures in

SHELTIE THE SHETLAND PONY
SHELTIE SAVES THE DAY
SHELTIE AND THE RUNAWAY
SHELTIE FINDS A FRIEND
SHELTIE TO THE RESCUE

Peter Clover was born and went to school in London. He was a storyboard artist and illustrator before he began to put words to his pictures. He enjoys painting, travelling, cooking and keeping fit, and lives on the coast in Somerset.

The Sheltie Series

Sheltie in Danger

Peter Clover

PUFFIN BOOKS

To Vicki and Mark

PUFFIN BOOKS

Published by the Penguin Group
Penguin Books Ltd, 80 Strand, London WC2R 0RL, England
Penguin Putnam Inc., 375 Hudson Street, New York, New York 10014, USA
Penguin Books Australia Ltd, Ringwood, Victoria, Australia
Penguin Books Canada Ltd, 10 Alcorn Avenue, Toronto, Ontario, Canada M4V 3B2
Penguin Books India (P) Ltd, 11 Community Centre, Panchsheel Park, New Delhi – 110 017, India
Penguin Books (NZ) Ltd, Cnr Rosedale and Airborne Roads, Albany, Auckland, New Zealand
Penguin Books (South Africa) (Pty) Ltd, 24 Sturdee Avenue, Rosebank 2196 South Africa

Penguin Books Ltd, Registered Offices: 80 Strand, London WC2R 0RL, England

www.penguin.com

First published 1997
10

Copyright © Working Partners Ltd, 1997
All rights reserved

Created by Working Partners Ltd, London W6 0HE

The moral right of the author/illustrator has been asserted

Filmset in 14/20 Palatino

Made and printed in England by Clays Ltd, St Ives plc

Chapter One

It was Saturday, and a cold and wintry morning in Little Applewood. Emma leaped out of bed and pulled on her dressing gown. She went over to the bedroom window and looked out on to the meadows and rolling hills of the countryside. Everything was crisp and white with the early morning frost.

Sheltie, Emma's Shetland pony,

stood by the fence in his paddock at the bottom of the garden. He stood there every morning, patiently waiting for Emma to appear at the window.

When Sheltie saw her he stamped his hoofs and blew a raspberry. Sheltie's warm breath made little white clouds in the frosty air. To Emma he looked like a big friendly dragon blowing smoke over the top of the wooden fence.

Emma got dressed in her warmest clothes. She put on two woolly jumpers and pulled on her new boots. A long red scarf, which her mum had knitted, hung across the back of a chair. Emma took the scarf and wrapped it around her neck. She felt cosy and warm, wrapped up against the cold.

Downstairs, Dad was laying out the breakfast things on the kitchen table. A saucepan of porridge was already bubbling on the stove, and the smell of sizzling bacon filled the cottage.

'Morning, Emma,' said Mum brightly. 'Breakfast in ten minutes.'

'OK, Mum,' Emma replied.

'Morny,' gurgled Joshua. Joshua was Emma's little brother. He was already sitting up at the kitchen table, playing with his spoon.

Outside, the air was crisp and fresh. Emma pulled the scarf up over her nose and went down to the paddock to give Sheltie his breakfast.

Sheltie didn't mind the cold weather at all. He had already grown his thick winter coat and was as warm as toast. Sheltie's mane and tail were so thick that any brush or comb became tangled up in the long straggly hair.

As Emma scooped Sheltie's pony mix into the feed manger, Sheltie grabbed one end of her scarf between his teeth and pulled.

Sheltie wouldn't let go of the scarf and Emma found herself in a game of tug-of-war and ended up with no scarf at all. Emma laughed as Sheltie galloped around the paddock, the scarf flying along behind him like a red banner.

When Sheltie came back he

dropped the scarf on the grass at
Emma's feet. It was wet and soggy at
one end.

'You are cheeky, Sheltie,' said
Emma. But she could never be cross
with him for long. Sheltie was such a
lovable little pony.

While Sheltie gobbled up his breakfast Emma put some hay in the rack on the back wall of the field shelter. Then she filled the drinking trough outside with water.

It was a lovely winter's day. The sky was clear blue and the sun shone brightly even though it was icy cold. The spiky grass was silver with frost.

Mum called to Emma from the back door and Emma hurried in for her breakfast.

'Bye, Sheltie. I'll see you later.'

Chapter Two

It was warm and cosy in the kitchen.
Emma sat down to a bowl of hot
porridge and a plate of bacon and
buttered toast.

Outside, a little robin landed on
the window sill and tapped on
the glass pane with its beak.
Joshua waved his spoon and the
little robin cocked his head to one
side.

'Can we give the robin some toast?' asked Emma.

'We can do better than that,' said Dad. 'I've been making a bird table so that we can feed all the birds right through the winter. It's nearly finished.'

'We can hang up nuts and put out bird seed and water,' said Mum.

'And bacon rind,' chirped Emma. 'Birds like that too!'

After breakfast Dad disappeared into his tool shed and set to work. He liked to make things in his shed. In no time at all he had finished the bird table. It even had perches and little pegs on which to hang bacon rind and bags of nuts.

They put the bird table down at the end of the garden. Sheltie stood looking over the top rail of the paddock fence, watching the birds feeding.

Sheltie wiggled his nose and showed his pony teeth in a funny grin. He wanted to eat some of the toast and breadcrumbs from the table, but it was too far away for him to reach.

Mum placed a shallow dish of water on the table and they all stood back as the robin came and took a drink.

The bird table could be easily seen through the kitchen window, so they went back inside and watched as all the other birds came to feed.

Emma brought out some paper and
coloured pencils, then sat down at
the kitchen table with Joshua, to
draw the robin and all his friends.

Later that morning, Sally came over
on Minnow, her pony. Sally was
Emma's best friend and they often
went riding together. The two girls

decided to ride over to Horseshoe
Pond and gather pine cones in the
wood behind Mr Brown's meadow.

Emma's mum was making table
decorations for the village craft shop
and had asked Emma to bring home
as many pine cones as she could find.

'The woods will be full of them,'
said Emma.

Sheltie and Minnow walked side
by side along the lane. Minnow was
bigger than Sheltie. Sheltie's head
only came up to Minnow's neck, but
he had strong little legs and could
trot just as fast as Minnow.

Sheltie liked Minnow and kept
nuzzling up to him with his nose as
they walked along.

The water in Horseshoe Pond was

like a mirror, still and silver with a thin covering of ice. The pond was in the shape of a giant horseshoe and, where its two ends almost met, there was a little hump of grass like an island.

A duck was sitting on the island, watching some others swimming about in a patch of water which hadn't yet quite frozen over.

'If it gets any colder the ducks won't have any water left to swim in at all,' said Emma.

'And if the ice gets really thick, we'll be able to go ice-skating,' said Sally.

Emma was thrilled at the idea of skating on Horseshoe Pond. She could hardly wait!

The two girls stood watching
the ducks for a while, then walked
the ponies up towards the
woods.

All the leaves had fallen from the
trees and there were pine cones
scattered everywhere. Emma and
Sally tied Sheltie and Minnow loosely
to a bare branch and left them
munching grass while they began
gathering up the cones.

In no time at all they had filled two
plastic carrier bags.

'Mum will be able to make heaps
of decorations with all these!' said
Emma.

Sheltie had found an enormous
cone beneath the tree and picked it
up carefully in his mouth. Emma

carried it home and let Sheltie
present it to Mum himself.

'What a clever pony you are,
Sheltie,' said Mum. 'It's the biggest
pine cone I've ever seen!'

Chapter Three

The very next day it snowed. When
Emma woke, her bedroom window
was white with frost. She pressed her
nose against the cold glass pane and
peered outside. Snowflakes the size
of ten-pence pieces drifted lazily
down from the sky and lay gently on
the ground.

Outside, everything was covered
with a thick blanket of snow. The

garden path had disappeared completely and Sheltie's paddock had turned from green to a glistening white. The distant hills had changed into white mountains of snow.

Sheltie stood at the fence, up to his knees in a drift of white, powdery snow. His long shaggy mane was frosted white, and beneath his fringe his eyes sparkled like diamonds.

Emma dressed quickly and hurried downstairs to look for her boots. They were where she had left them, by the kitchen door.

Feeding Sheltie that morning was more fun than usual. The snowfall had made Sheltie friskier than ever and he was in a playful mood.

Each time Emma bent over, Sheltie

nudged her with his muzzle and sent
Emma headlong into the snow.

Emma made snowballs and chased
Sheltie around the paddock. Sheltie
thought this was great fun and tried

to eat all the snowballs that Emma
threw at him.

Mum and Dad came out of the
cottage with Joshua, to watch the
snowball fight. They stood by the
fence as Sheltie galloped round and
round the paddock, chasing the
snowballs and falling snowflakes.

'I'll make you a sleigh,' said Dad.
'If this snow keeps up, Sheltie will be
able to pull it along and give you
some lovely rides.'

Sheltie seemed to like this idea and he swished his tail to and fro. He shook the snow from his mane and blew a white cloud of steam from his nostrils.

Chapter Four

The snow fell for most of Sunday. By late afternoon Little Applewood was completely covered in a crisp white blanket.

Everything shone white as far as you could see. All the trees glistened with fresh white flakes. The cottage rooftops were thick with snow and their chimney pots wore tall white hats.

Sheltie left deep tracks in the snow wherever he went. Emma put down some more straw on the floor of Sheltie's field shelter to keep his feet dry.

By half-past four it was getting dark and Emma was helping Mum to make the tea. Dad sat at the kitchen table with a pencil and paper, working out how to turn the old toboggan he had found in his shed into a sleigh for Sheltie to pull.

Emma was looking forward to riding on the sleigh and so was Joshua. Being pulled along by Sheltie would be such great fun.

The next morning was the start of Emma's half-term holiday from

school. Dad had taken the week off
from work too, to do some odd jobs
around the cottage and to look after
Emma and Joshua whenever Mum
was busy at the village craft shop.

Dad had disappeared into his shed
to start work on the sleigh. It was
going to be a surprise, so Emma
wasn't allowed to peep until it was
finished.

As Emma fed Sheltie his breakfast
she could hear banging and sawing
coming from inside the shed. Dad
was fixing two shafts on to the
toboggan. She told Sheltie that he
was going to have a sleigh to pull,
and he seemed very excited.

Mum and Joshua put some
breadcrumbs out on the bird table,

then went into the paddock to help Emma and Sheltie make a snowman.

First Emma made a big snowball. Then she rolled it around the paddock until it grew bigger and bigger. When it was big enough to be the snowman's body Emma rolled it across to the gate. Sheltie helped and gave it a push with his nose.

Then they made a smaller snowball for the snowman's head. Mum put the head on top of the body and pushed a carrot into the snowball to make a long nose. Sheltie was very naughty and tried to pull the carrot out. Sheltie liked carrots and wanted to eat it, so Emma had to go and fetch him another one as a treat.

They made eyes for the snowman

with two small lumps of coal and a
smiley mouth from little stones. Then
Emma wrapped her scarf around its
neck and Mum popped a woolly hat
on top of the snowman's head. It
made him look quite grand.

Sheltie cocked his head to one side and looked at the snowman. Then he pawed at the snow with his hoof and wanted to play. But the snowman didn't move. He wasn't as much fun as Emma, so Sheltie gave him a hard nudge and knocked his head off. Then he grabbed the carrot nose and galloped off with it across the paddock.

Chapter Five

Later that morning, Sally came over
on Minnow and the two girls rode
over to Mr Brown's meadow to see if
Horseshoe Pond had frozen over
completely.

It had! When they got there,
Mr Brown was standing in the
middle of the thick ice, where
the pond curved. He saw the two
girls on their ponies and jumped up

and down on the ice to test its strength.

'I expect you two will be up here with your skates now!' said Mr Brown. 'It's rock solid.' He gave a friendly wave, then slipped and sat down on the ice with a bump.

Emma and Sally started to laugh. Mr Brown was laughing too and Sheltie gave a funny snort.

'I think I'll leave the skating to you youngsters,' he said as he pulled himself to his feet.

Emma and Sally jumped down from their saddles and landed almost up to their knees in a drift of soft snow. They left Sheltie and Minnow under the sycamore tree. A patch of green grass was still showing through the white snow where the ground was sheltered beneath the tree branches.

Sheltie and Minnow lowered their heads and munched at the grass.

Emma stepped carefully out on to the ice. It was very slippery and difficult to walk on at first. Sally took a run at it and did a big slide across the surface of the pond.

'This is brilliant!' said Sally. 'I can't wait to get my ice-skates on.'

Emma didn't have any ice-skates, but Sally had a spare pair at home. She said that she would teach Emma to skate, so the two friends trotted on their ponies all the way to Fox Hall Manor and back to fetch them.

When they returned, Horseshoe Pond shone and glistened like

polished glass. Emma and Sally sat on the snowy bank and put on their skates. Sheltie and Minnow stood by watching. Sheltie was very interested in what was going on.

When Sally stood up on the ice and went gliding across the pond, Sheltie's ears pricked up in surprise and he made a funny snorting noise.

Although Emma had never been ice-skating before, she was very good on roller skates. The slippery ice felt odd beneath her feet and she was a bit wobbly at first.

Sally held Emma's hand and led her on to the ice and around the pond. When Sheltie saw Emma skating, he trotted over to the edge of the pond and put one hoof on the ice.

'No, Sheltie,' said Emma. 'You can't skate. Stay there and watch.'

But Sheltie didn't want to stay and watch. He wanted to skate across the ice like Emma.

Emma hoped that Sheltie was going to behave. She knew he was very determined. Minnow was a very quiet pony, but he did tend to copy everything that Sheltie did, and the last thing that Emma wanted was two ponies skidding on the ice.

Sheltie calmed down and stepped back from the pond. He watched Emma skating, from beneath the tree.

Emma learned very quickly and was soon skating on her own, round and round Horseshoe Pond. Then she slipped and fell down on the ice with her legs waving in the air.

Sally laughed and went to help Emma back up on to her feet. But the ice was so slippery and the two girls were laughing so much that they

both ended up in a heap, sprawled
across the icy surface of the pond.

Sheltie thought that this looked
like great fun and wanted to join in.
He dashed down on to the ice and
slid on all fours right across the pond
to the other side.

Sheltie went so fast that when he reached the far bank he gave a little hop and landed back on the grass.

'Look at Sheltie,' laughed Sally. 'He can skate!'

'The world's first skating pony,' said Emma.

Sheltie looked more surprised than anyone. He glanced back across the ice with a puzzled look as if to say, 'How did I do that?'

Sheltie kept away from the ice from then on. He was happy to stand with Minnow and watch.

The two girls continued skating until it was time to go home for their lunch.

Chapter Six

Dad was sitting in the kitchen having a mug of hot tea and looking very pleased with himself. He told Emma that Sheltie's sleigh was almost finished.

'Let's hope the snow doesn't melt overnight,' said Dad, 'then you and Sheltie can have some real fun tomorrow.'

Emma helped Mum to clear away

the plates after lunch and wash and dry the dishes. Then she decided to ride Sheltie back over to Horseshoe Pond. Emma wanted to practise her skating again so that she would be as good as Sally.

Sheltie stood by the edge of the pond and watched as Emma sat on the snowy bank and put on Sally's spare ice-skates.

Emma was a lot better already and didn't wobble half as much as before. Each time she skated round the pond and passed Sheltie she gave him a little wave.

And each time Emma went by Sheltie tossed his head and gave a little snort.

Then a terrible thing happened.

The ice wasn't as thick as Emma had thought. Around the edge of the pond the ice was as solid as a rock. But further in, where the water was deeper, there was a patch of ice that was thinner than the rest. Even Mr Brown hadn't seen it.

The first time Emma had skated across that spot, the ice had cracked a little but not enough for Emma to notice. But the second time, the ice gave way completely and Emma fell right through into the freezing water beneath.

Emma let out a scream as she fell. Although the water only came up to just past her waist, it was icy cold. Her feet got stuck in the muddy goo on the pond bed and the cold water took her breath away.

'Help, Sheltie! Help!' cried Emma.

Sheltie was quick to act. The moment he saw Emma disappear through the hole in the ice he raced to her rescue.

Sheltie's hoofs slipped and skidded on the ice as he dashed forward on to the pond.

Although Sheltie was only a small pony, he was very heavy, and his weight made the thin ice around the hole crack and give way.

As Sheltie reached Emma, the ice broke away completely beneath him and he plunged down into the water beside her.

Emma grabbed Sheltie's mane and

managed to scramble up on to the
ice. Emma was soaked right through,
but she was safely out of the freezing
water and stood on the solid ice
away from the hole.

But Sheltie's feet were stuck. He

couldn't move and was standing up to his neck in the icy water. He struggled to climb back up on to the frozen surface, but he couldn't. Poor Sheltie remained trapped as he whinnied and blew with loud snorts. The more he struggled, the more stuck he became.

'Hang on, Sheltie!' cried Emma. She was shaking with fright. 'I'll go for help.'

Emma pulled off the skates and ran as fast as she could back to the cottage.

Chapter Seven

Emma was sobbing as she ran. By the time she burst through the back door into the kitchen her eyes were red and puffy.

Her clothes were soaked right through and her legs were covered with slimy mud. She was shaking and crying as she fell into Mum's arms.

'Emma!' cried Mum. 'What on earth has happened?' She put her arms around Emma and pushed the wet hair away from her eyes.

Emma was so upset she could hardly speak. 'It's . . . it's . . . Sheltie. He's fallen into the pond . . . We've got to help him. The ice broke and I fell in. Sheltie saved me but now he's stuck. Oh, Mum! It's freezing. Poor Sheltie will freeze to death. We've got to get him out! We've got to help him!'

Emma managed to blurt out the story in one breath, then she hugged Mum tightly. She couldn't stop herself from shaking.

Dad flew down the stairs. He had heard what had happened and rushed out into the hall to get his coat.

'I'll fetch the car,' said Dad. 'There

are ropes in the boot.' He told Mum to telephone Mr Brown and ask him to come to the pond with his tractor. Then he ran outside to the car and sped off up the lane.

Mum made the phone call to Mr Brown, then got Emma out of her wet clothes and ran a hot bath.

Emma sat by the kitchen range wrapped in a thick blanket, warming herself by the open fire. She was so worried. All she could think of was poor Sheltie stuck in the freezing cold pond.

Dad drove the car right through the double gates and across the meadow to Horseshoe Pond. The car tyres left dark tracks in the white snow.

As Dad jumped out of the car he saw Sheltie's head sticking out above the ice in the middle of the pond.

'It's all right, Sheltie!' he called out. 'Hang on, boy. We'll soon get you out of there!'

Sheltie let out a feeble snort. He was freezing cold and feeling very weak. Struggling to get out of the pond had made his feet well and truly stuck in the gooey mud. Sheltie was tired and very frightened.

Dad took a rope from the car and made a loop at one end. But he couldn't see how he could tie the rope to Sheltie to pull him out.

It was hopeless. And poor Sheltie was unable to climb up out of the hole on his own.

Across the snowy meadow came
Mr Brown, chugging along in his
tractor. He had several long planks of
wood in the back and laid them across
the ice to stand on. Then Mr Brown

took a sledgehammer and began smashing the ice. He made a rough little path from the hole to the near edge of the pond.

'I've called the fire brigade,' said Mr Brown. 'They should be here any minute.'

Suddenly a blue flashing light appeared. Emma's dad called out and waved the fire engine over to the pond.

Carefully, the firemen reversed the engine right up to the edge of the snowy bank. A strong ladder swung out over the pond, and Emma's dad watched as they passed a cable through the rungs and attached it to a winch.

One fireman had jumped into the

freezing water and was talking
quietly to Sheltie.

'Don't worry, boy. We'll soon have
you out,' he said.

Sheltie answered with a weak
whinny.

The fireman fitted a sling around Sheltie's tummy, then hooked the sling to the cable overhead. He stayed with Sheltie as the winch droned and began to turn.

There was a squelching noise as Sheltie's hoofs came free of the muddy goo and weeds. Then, slowly, the little pony was lifted clear of the icy water and gently lowered on to the bank.

Sheltie was puffing and blowing with fright, but at last he was standing safely on dry land.

Chapter Eight

Poor Sheltie was covered in sticky
mud. His coat and mane were
plastered to his body with icy water.
Emma's little pony was shivering
with fright, but he was safe.

Mr Brown took some blankets from
the tractor and threw them over
Sheltie.

'Best try to get most of the water
out and dry him off,' said Mr Brown.

Dad rubbed Sheltie's face and
mane with a blanket while Mr Brown
set to work on Sheltie's back. Then
both men started drying his sides
and legs. Sheltie's tail was sopping
wet. The blankets were soaked,
and the little pony was still
dripping.

'Poor thing must be frozen through
to his bones,' said Dad.

'You should get him home as
quickly as you can,' said Mr Brown.
'Get him moving so that he warms
up a bit. And put another dry blanket
on him before you walk him back.'

Sheltie's nose was ice cold.

'Poor Sheltie,' said Dad. He stroked
Sheltie's head, then replaced the wet
blanket with a dry one and led the

little pony off across the white
meadow and up the lane.

'I'll come back for the car later,'
Dad called over his shoulder to the
farmer.

Sheltie's legs were wobbly, but he
kept walking until they arrived at the
paddock. Dad put Sheltie into his
field shelter, then raced to the cottage
to fetch more dry blankets and some
old towels.

Emma had dried out now and
wanted to help. When she saw
Sheltie she threw her arms around
his neck and gave him a big hug.

Sheltie sneezed, then closed his
eyes and lowered his head.

'Come on, Emma,' said Dad. 'Let's
get him nice and dry.'

Mum and Joshua came out to the
stable with two mugs of hot tea.
Mum helped to dry Sheltie off with
one of the towels.

Sheltie's thick woolly coat was

getting drier by the minute, but he was still cold and shivering. Dad put lots of straw down on the floor and threw a nice dry blanket over him. Then he packed some more straw underneath Sheltie's blanket for extra warmth.

'We can't do any more,' said Dad. 'Let's hope Sheltie dries out quickly on his own.' He went inside to telephone Mr Thorne, the vet, and asked him to come over to take a look at Sheltie.

When the vet arrived it was already pitch dark. The sky looked as though it was full of snow again and the temperature had dropped to freezing.

Sheltie looked sad and miserable.

'He's had quite a scare,' said Mr Thorne. 'And the poor thing is frozen right through. We can only hope that he warms up and doesn't get ill.'

The vet gave Sheltie an injection and said that they should keep a close eye on him. He would pop over in the morning to see how Sheltie was feeling.

'He's a tough little Shetland,' Mr Thorne said. 'He's used to the cold weather. But you must keep him warm and hope for the best.'

Mum stroked Emma's hair.

'Don't worry, Emma,' she said. 'We'll look after Sheltie. He'll be all right.'

Chapter Nine

Emma didn't sleep a wink all night. She kept thinking about poor Sheltie. She couldn't bear the thought of him being unwell. If anything should happen to him . . .

Emma sobbed into her pillow.

The next morning, Emma got dressed quicker than ever, and ran down to the paddock.

It had been snowing in the night and the snow was even thicker. All the tracks and footprints from the previous day had disappeared. Emma raced across the paddock to the field shelter.

Sheltie looked awful. He wasn't perky at all. He just stood there, staring straight ahead, hardly moving.

Emma whispered Sheltie's name and stroked his neck. He was sweating slightly and his coat felt damp. He gave a sneeze and Emma saw that his nose was runny and his eyes were watery.

Emma pulled some hay from the rack and offered it in her hand. Slowly, Sheltie took the feed and

tried to eat, but after a moment the hay just fell to the floor.

Emma put a scoop of pony mix into the manger, but poor Sheltie wasn't interested. He gave another sneeze and started to cough.

Emma ran back to the cottage to fetch Mum.

*

Mr Thorne, the vet, came back just after breakfast. He examined Sheltie and took the little pony's temperature.

'I'm afraid Sheltie has a fever.' Mr Thorne looked worried. 'As I suspected yesterday, he's caught a bad cold.'

'Is there anything we can do?' asked Mum.

'We can only hope it doesn't develop into something much worse,' said the vet.

Emma looked up at Mum.

'Sheltie will be all right, won't he?'

'We'll do whatever we can,' said Mum. 'We'll look after him. We'll do our best. We all will.'

Dad and Joshua nodded.

The vet gave Sheltie another injection and said that all they could do was to keep him warm and quiet.

Sheltie was a very poorly little pony.

Sheltie's field shelter was closed in on three sides but one wall was open and looked out across the paddock.

Mr Thorne said that they should pile bales of straw across the wide opening to keep out the cold wind. And he gave Mum a small bottle of brown liquid and said that they should add a few drops to a bowl of hot water so that Sheltie could breathe in the fumes. It would help Sheltie's cough and make it easier for him to breathe.

'Make up a bran mash to keep up

his strength,' added Mr Thorne. 'Try to get him to eat. Spoon-feed him if you have to. And bathe his eyes with warm water.'

Emma swallowed hard. She was very upset.

Dad spoke quietly. 'Is there a good chance of Sheltie getting better?' he asked.

'We can only hope for the best,' said the vet. 'Sheltie is going to need lots of love and care.'

Emma stood up straight. Sheltie had saved her life. She was determined to nurse him back to health.

Chapter Ten

'Right,' said Dad. 'Let's get those bales of straw. I'll drive over to the farm straight away.'

While Dad went to fetch the bales, Emma laid down a thick bedding of straw all around Sheltie and packed fresh, dry straw underneath his blanket.

Poor Sheltie stood with his head held low. His ears, normally alert and pointy, lay floppy against his head and he looked very sick. Then he let out a loud sneeze and began to cough.

Dad came back with twelve bales of straw and Emma helped to pile them across the open end of the shelter. It was much warmer inside now.

Mum appeared, with Joshua trailing behind her. 'Here's that bowl of hot water,' she said.

The drops of liquid in the hot water gave off a lovely smelling vapour. Emma took a deep breath. It was like strong peppermint.

Emma held the bowl near Sheltie and the steam drifted up towards him. Sheltie's nostrils twitched at

the peppermint smell and it seemed
to help him to breathe more easily.
The vet had also said that they

should bathe Sheltie's eyes, so Mum
took some cotton wool and another
bowl of warm water. Emma watched
as Mum carefully wiped his eyes and
lashes.

Dad changed the blanket for a nice
dry one that had been warming on
the kitchen range. They made Sheltie
as comfortable as they could.

'Poor, poor Sheltie,' whispered
Emma as she gently stroked the little
pony's mane. She felt really sad
seeing Sheltie like this and felt a pain
like a knot in her tummy.

In the afternoon, Sally came riding
over on Minnow. When she saw
Emma's face she knew immediately
that something was wrong. Sally

hadn't heard about the accident.

'What is it, Emma?' she asked.

Emma swallowed hard, gulping back her tears. She really was trying to be brave.

'It's Sheltie,' she said. 'I fell through the ice on Horseshoe Pond and Sheltie saved me. But now he's very ill.' The words seemed to stick in Emma's throat.

Sally could tell by Emma's voice that it was serious.

'Is Sheltie going to be all right?' she asked.

Emma's face crumpled. 'I hope so, Sally,' she said.

Sally put her arm around Emma and listened to everything that had happened.

'Oh, poor Sheltie,' said Sally. 'Can I do anything to help?'

Emma shook her head. She had never felt this sad before.

Chapter Eleven

That same afternoon, Dad brought
out his spare car battery and a special
attachment to put up a light in
Sheltie's field shelter. He fitted a
heating bulb into the light socket, to
give Sheltie some extra warmth.

Emma and Mum made a bran
mash just like Mr Thorne had said
and spoon-fed Sheltie with the
mixture.

Sheltie was normally so lively and loved his food, but now he didn't seem to want to eat at all. Emma offered him fresh water in a plastic bucket, but Sheltie just stared at it with his head low.

'He looks worse than ever,' said Emma.

The next day was just as bad. Emma didn't like leaving Sheltie out in the shelter all on his own overnight, but there was nothing else they could do.

The snow had settled and it was very cold. Sweeping white drifts had blown up outside against the stable walls and the air inside was cold and damp.

The heated light was left on all the

time and Emma refreshed the steaming bowl of peppermint vapour every hour. It all helped, but Sheltie was still very poorly.

Emma spent every minute of the long day with Sheltie. She took books into the stable and read aloud to the little pony so that he could hear her voice and know that she was there.

Emma told Sheltie how the little robin had come for his breakfast at the bird table. And she told the little pony all about the wonderful sleigh that Dad had made for him.

'It's even got your name painted on the side,' said Emma.

Sheltie listened to everything that Emma said and breathed in the

vapour from the bowl that Emma
had placed at his feet.

Sally came to visit again. She stood
outside the field shelter clutching a
plastic bag.

'I couldn't think of anything else to

bring you,' said Sally, pulling out a
pony magazine and some comics. 'I
brought these as well.' Sally handed
Emma a packet of peppermints.
'They're for Sheltie when he gets
better.'

Sally stayed for lunch. But no one
really felt like eating anything.
Everyone was very upset and waiting
for Mr Thorne's next visit.

When the vet arrived, they all went down to the paddock. There was a terrible shock waiting for them when they stepped into the shelter. Sheltie was lying down on his side on the straw. He was making funny noises and his ribs heaved each time he took a breath.

Sheltie wasn't getting better. In fact, he looked much worse.

Chapter Twelve

The vet was very worried. He put his bag down and examined the little pony.

'I'm afraid Sheltie has taken a turn for the worse,' he said. 'There's nothing more that we can do.'

Sheltie turned his head slightly and opened his eyes to look up at Emma. He whinnied softly, then closed his eyes again.

'Sheltie, Sheltie,' sobbed Emma. She threw herself on to the straw and put her arms around Sheltie's neck.

'You've done everything you can, Emma,' said Mr Thorne. 'It's up to Sheltie now. I'm very sorry.'

Dad took Emma indoors. She and Sally were so upset. Emma's mum took Sally home in the car.

That evening, nobody felt like eating a big meal, so Mum just made some sandwiches and they all sat at the kitchen table.

At bedtime, Mum tucked up Emma with an extra blanket and sat with her until she fell asleep.

But Emma didn't stay asleep for

long. Her thoughts were filled with dreams of poor Sheltie.

When Mum and Dad had gone to bed, Emma got up. She put on her warmest clothes and an extra woolly jumper. She wrapped the spare blanket around her shoulders. Then she tiptoed downstairs to the kitchen and filled a fresh bowl with hot water.

Emma opened the back door quietly and crunched through the snow down to the paddock to visit Sheltie.

The little pony was still lying down, but he looked peaceful, as though he were sleeping soundly.

Emma knelt down and stroked Sheltie's neck. His coat didn't feel damp with sweat any more. It felt quite dry, and his ears twitched as she spoke softly to him.

'You've got to pull through, Sheltie. You've got to.'

Sheltie gave a little sigh and opened his eyes.

Emma put the peppermint-smelling drops into the bowl of hot water. Then she thought she would try Sheltie with a little food. She took a spoon and managed to feed him some bran mash, a little at a time. Sheltie seemed to know that he had to eat in order to get better.

'Good boy. Good Sheltie,' said Emma.

Each time Sheltie took a mouthful, Emma felt a little more hope. But the

small, sick pony lying on the bed of straw was not like the Sheltie she knew. It was hard to imagine him racing around the paddock, looking for mischief.

Emma placed the bowl of hot water by Sheltie's head so that he could breathe in the vapour through the rest of the night. She covered him with her blanket and snuggled up against the little Shetland pony.

She lay her head against his neck for a little while before she crept over to the far corner of the shelter and fell asleep, curled up on the soft straw.

Chapter Thirteen

When Emma woke the next morning,
at first she didn't know where she
was. The sun was rising slowly over
the back meadow and the field shelter
was filled with a soft golden light.

Emma blinked the sleep from her
eyes. She heard a soft whicker.
Sheltie!

Emma sat up quickly. She could
hardly believe what she saw.

The little Shetland pony was standing up on his feet. He seemed a little unsteady, but he was standing all the same. His eyes looked brighter and he greeted her with a little snort.

As Emma jumped up, Sheltie gave
a tiny sneeze. Then he swished his
tail and made the funny noises he
always did when he was hungry and
waiting for his breakfast.

Sheltie was really happy to see
Emma. And Emma had never felt so
happy in her life. She was so happy
she wrapped her arms around
Sheltie's neck and gave him a big,
long hug.

Emma ran outside. Everything as
far as she could see was still covered
white with snow. The countryside
was quiet and peaceful. All the usual
sounds seemed to be muffled by the
thick blanket of snow.

Emma raced as fast as her legs
could carry her. She ran through the

snow and across the paddock. She was in such a hurry to tell Mum and Dad, Emma didn't have time to open the gate, so she climbed over it and ran up the garden to the cottage.

When Emma burst into the kitchen, Mum was getting ready for breakfast. She was very surprised to see Emma up so early.

Emma didn't need to say anything. The delighted look on her face said it all. Sheltie was going to be all right!

Over the next few days, Sheltie got stronger and stronger. He began eating on his own again and soon looked like his old self. There was no more coughing, no more sneezing and no more runny eyes.

Mr Thorne came over to check on Sheltie and gave the little Shetland pony a clean bill of health.

'Sheltie's made a remarkable recovery,' said the vet. 'And I'm certain that it has a lot to do with all the loving care and attention that you've been giving him, Emma.'

Emma beamed a big smile. She was so glad that Sheltie was fit and well again.

'No doubt Sheltie will be wanting to race around in the paddock soon,' said Mr Thorne.

'But it's still very snowy,' said Emma. 'Will Sheltie be all right?'

'Of course he will,' said the vet. 'Sheltie is fine now. He's a tough little Shetland pony.'

Sheltie puffed out his chest and blew a raspberry. Just like he always did.

Chapter Fourteen

It was Saturday morning and the sun shone brightly in the frosty, pale-blue sky. Although it was more than a week later, the white snow still gleamed like icing sugar across the paddock.

Sheltie stood pawing at a soft drift. He was blowing and snorting and eager to get going.

Dad had made a special harness to

fit around Sheltie's chest. And the
two long shafts which were fixed to
the sleigh were strapped in place.

Emma sat on the little wooden seat
holding on to the sides. There were
no reins to steer with. Dad was going
to lead from the front.

'Ready, Emma?'

Emma grinned and nodded.

'Come on, Sheltie,' said Dad. 'Race you around the paddock.' And they were off.

Sheltie trotted easily along, pulling the sleigh smoothly behind him. Dad was puffing like an old train. And Emma was giggling and calling for Sheltie to go faster.

Riding in the sleigh was great fun, especially when they turned corners. Then the sleigh would shoot out to the side really fast.

Emma gave a little scream whenever this happened, and Sheltie answered with a loud snort.

In the afternoon, Sally came over to play. Sheltie was showing off in front of Minnow and pulling the sleigh as fast as his little legs would carry him. Emma was leading Sheltie now and pulling Sally in the sleigh, all around the paddock.

Mum and Dad and Joshua were watching through the kitchen window. Emma was racing in front of Sheltie, holding the lead rope and laughing.

Sheltie was trying to grab the packet of peppermints sticking out of Emma's jacket pocket.

When they stopped, Sheltie nudged Emma headlong into a pile of soft snow.

Sally jumped out of the sleigh and joined Emma in a frosty heap. The two girls had a fit of the giggles and showered each other with snow.

Then Sheltie pinched the packet of peppermints from Emma's pocket and ran off, with the empty sleigh zigzagging behind him.

'He's so funny, isn't he?' laughed Sally.

Sheltie was blowing loud raspberries as he ran.

'I'll give him funny when I catch him!' giggled Emma. And she chased Sheltie all over the paddock.

It was good to have her dearest friend back to his old self again.

If you like making friends, fun, excitement and adventure, then you'll love

The little pony with the big heart!

Sheltie is the lovable little Shetland pony with a big personality. He is cheeky, full of fun and has a heart of gold. His owner, Emma, knew that she and Sheltie would be best friends as soon as she saw him. She could tell that he thought so too by the way his brown eyes twinkled beneath his big, bushy mane. When Emma, her mum and dad and little brother, Joshua, first moved to Little Applewood, she thought that she might not like living there. But life is never dull with Sheltie around. He is full of mischief and he and Emma have lots of exciting adventures together.

Share Sheltie and Emma's adventures in:

SHELTIE THE SHETLAND PONY
SHELTIE SAVES THE DAY
SHELTIE AND THE RUNAWAY
SHELTIE FINDS A FRIEND
SHELTIE TO THE RESCUE

READ MORE IN PUFFIN

For children of all ages, Puffin represents quality and variety – the very best in publishing today around the world.

For complete information about books available from Puffin – and Penguin – and how to order them, contact us at the appropriate address below. Please note that for copyright reasons the selection of books varies from country to country.

On the worldwide web: www.puffin.co.uk

In the United Kingdom: Please write to *Dept. EP, Penguin Books Ltd, Bath Road, Harmondsworth, West Drayton, Middlesex UB7 0DA*

In the United States: Please write to *Consumer Sales, Penguin USA, P.O. Box 999, Dept. 17109, Bergenfield, New Jersey 07621-0120*. VISA and MasterCard holders call 1-800-253-6476 to order Penguin titles

In Canada: Please write to *Penguin Books Canada Ltd, 10 Alcorn Avenue, Suite 300, Toronto, Ontario M4V 3B2*

In Australia: Please write to *Penguin Books Australia Ltd, P.O. Box 257, Ringwood, Victoria 3134*

In New Zealand: Please write to *Penguin Books (NZ) Ltd, Private Bag 102902, North Shore Mail Centre, Auckland 10*

In India: Please write to *Penguin Books India Pvt Ltd, 706 Eros Apartments, 56 Nehru Place, New Delhi 110 019*

In the Netherlands: Please write to *Penguin Books Netherlands bv, Postbus 3507, NL-1001 AH Amsterdam*

In Germany: Please write to *Penguin Books Deutschland GmbH, Metzlerstrasse 26, 60594 Frankfurt am Main*

In Spain: Please write to *Penguin Books S. A., Bravo Murillo 19, 1° B, 28015 Madrid*

In Italy: Please write to *Penguin Italia s.r.l., Via Felice Casati 20, I-20124 Milano*

In France: Please write to *Penguin France S. A., 17 rue Lejeune, F-31000 Toulouse*

In Japan: Please write to *Penguin Books Japan, Ishikiribashi Building, 2-5-4, Suido, Bunkyo-ku, Tokyo 112*

In South Africa: Please write to *Longman Penguin Southern Africa (Pty) Ltd, Private Bag X08, Bertsham 2013*